YES DEAR

This leaf belongs to

First published in hardback in Great Britain by
HarperCollins Publishers Ltd in 1992
10 9 8 7 6 5 4 3 2
ISBN: 0 00 184643-4 (Hardback)
First published in Great Britain
in Picture Lions in 1993
10 9 8 7 6 5 4 3 2 1
ISBN: 0 00 664300-0 (Picture Lions)
Picture Lions is an imprint of the Children's Division,
part of HarperCollins Publishers Limited,
77-85 Fulham Palace Road, Hammersmith,
London W6 8JB

The author and illustrator assert the moral right to
be identified as the author and illustrator of the work.
Text copyright © Diana Wynne Jones 1992
Illustrations copyright © Graham Philpot 1992

A CIP catalogue record for this title
is available from the British Library.

Printed in Hong Kong
This book is set in 24/31 Goudy

YES DEAR

Diana Wynne Jones
Illustrated by Graham Philpot

Collins
An Imprint of HarperCollins*Publishers*

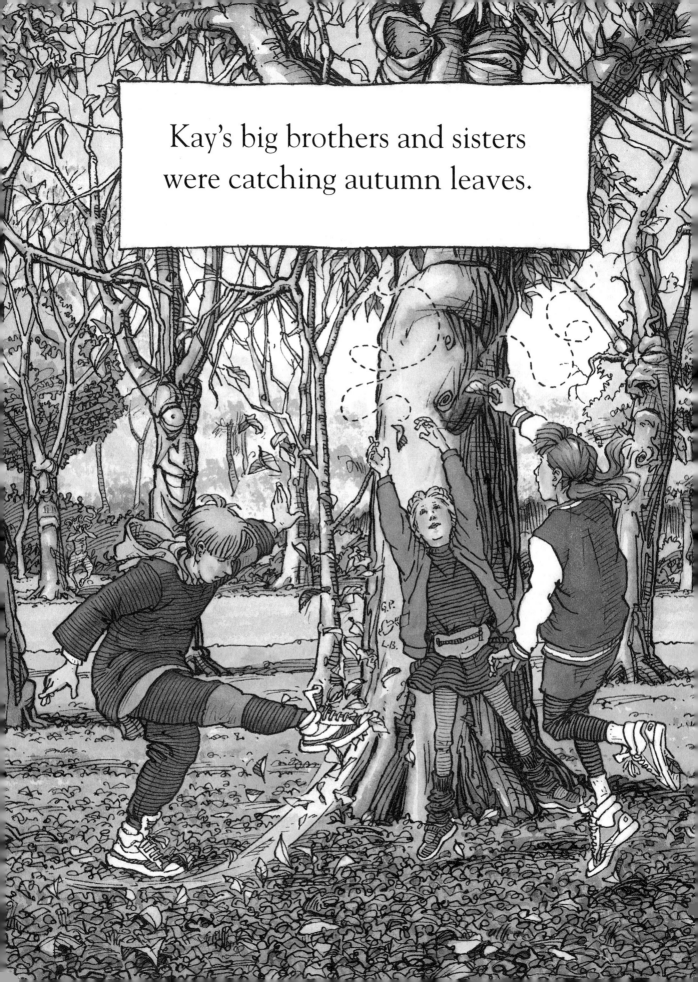

Kay's big brothers and sisters were catching autumn leaves.

Kay tried to catch one too,
and tried, and tried, and caught one.
It was bright and yellow and shiny.

"Look!" Kay shouted.
"I've caught a magic golden leaf!"
"Yes dear," Kay's brothers and sisters said kindly.
"Run along and play and don't bother us now."

"I *know* it's a magic leaf,"
Kay said.
"I shall wish that my sand pies
and my sand cakes
and my sand pancakes were real."

And they were.
Then Kay made sand pizzas
and sand ice-creams and sand sandwiches,
and they were real too.
"I shall tell Mum," said Kay.

Kay found Mum in a flowerbed.
"Mum, Mum!" Kay shouted.
"Look at my magic golden leaf.
It made my sand pies real!"

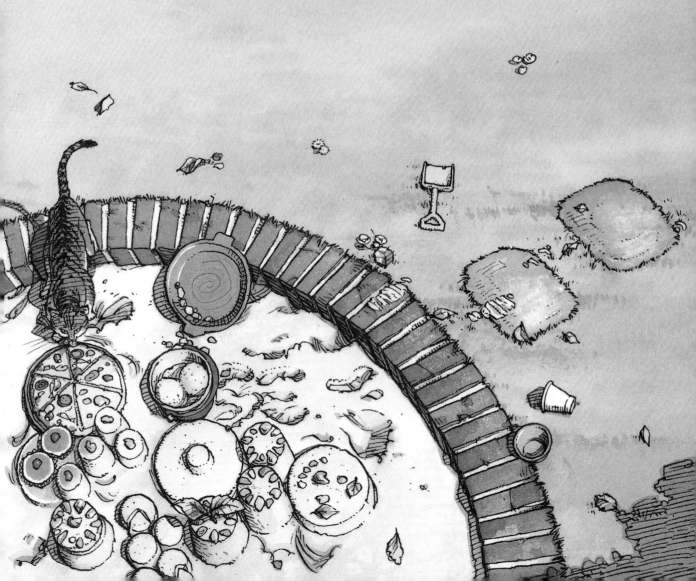

"Yes dear," Mum said kindly.
"Run along and play
and don't bother me now.
I'm trying to do the garden."

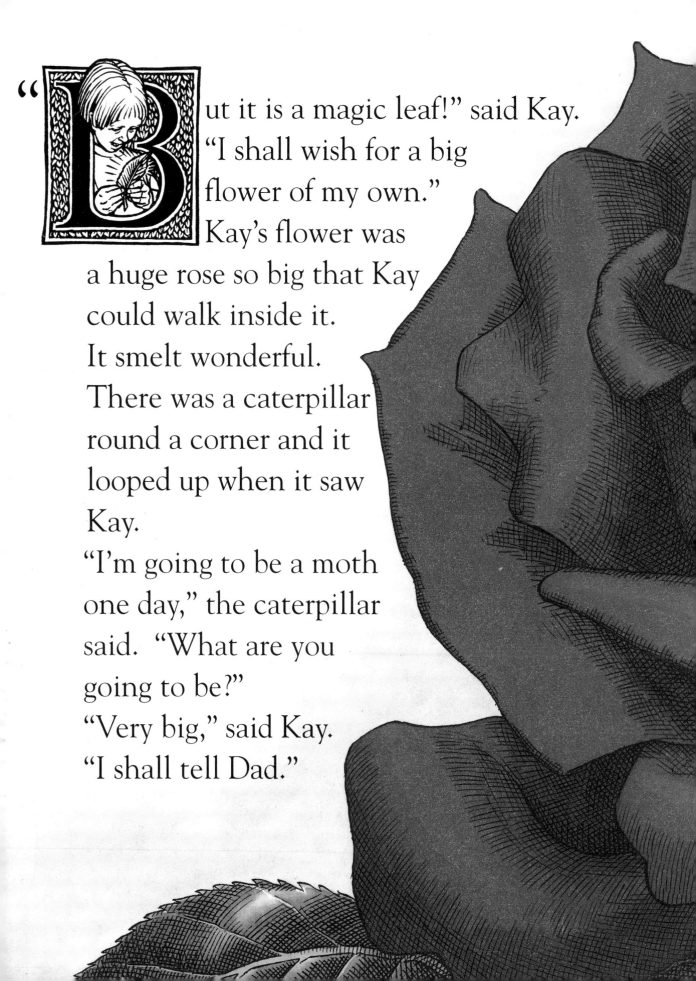

"But it is a magic leaf!" said Kay. "I shall wish for a big flower of my own."

Kay's flower was a huge rose so big that Kay could walk inside it. It smelt wonderful. There was a caterpillar round a corner and it looped up when it saw Kay.

"I'm going to be a moth one day," the caterpillar said. "What are you going to be?"

"Very big," said Kay.

"I shall tell Dad."

Kay found Dad in the kitchen
making a lot of bubbles in the sink.
"Dad, Dad!" Kay shouted. .
"Look at my magic golden leaf!
It made a big rose
with a caterpillar inside
and real sand pies."
"Yes dear," Dad said kindly.
"Run away and play and
don't bother me now.
The washing machine has
broken and I'm trying to
wash my socks."

"But it is a magic leaf!" said Kay. "I shall wish for bubbles now."
Kay's bubbles came in crowds. Some were like rainbows, some were like jewels, some had castles in, and dragons, and ships, and towers, and faces.

When Kay
poked them
they went
Blop!
and burst.
"I must tell someone,"
said Kay.

Kay's sisters were in the bedroom by then
playing dressing-up with the bedspreads.
"Look at my magic leaf!" Kay shouted.
"It made big coloured bubbles
and a rose with a caterpillar inside,
and real sand pies."
"Yes dear," Kay's sisters said kindly.
"Run away and play
and don't bother us now.
We are being
kings and queens."

"But it is a magic leaf!" said Kay. "I shall wish to be dressed up too." Kay's clothes were ten times finer than any bedspread.

They were silk and satin with knobby jewels and feathery lace and rattling gold net and Kay wore a spiked crown and pointed shoes with cold buckles.

The patchwork quilt turned into Kay's kingdom and stretched way into the blue distance.

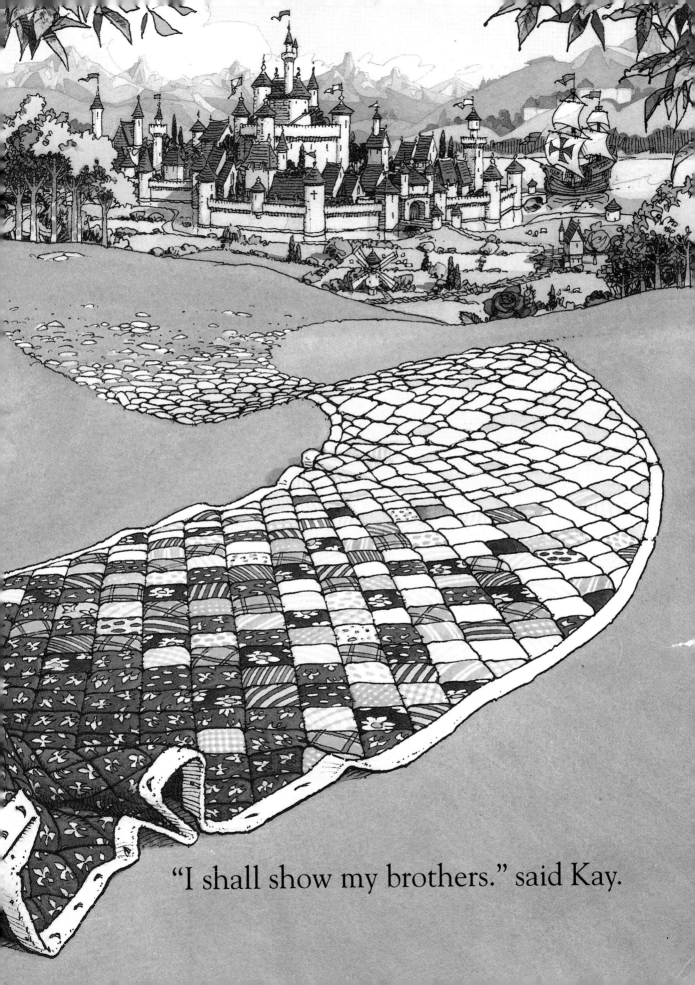

"I shall show my brothers." said Kay.

Kay's brothers were twanging guitars
and thumping drums.
"Look, look!" Kay shouted.
"My magic leaf has made me fine clothes now,
and coloured bubbles,
and a rose with a caterpillar inside
and real sand pies."
"Yes dear," Kay's brothers
said quite kindly.
"Run away and play and
don't bother us now.
We are busy
with our music."

"**B**ut it is a magic leaf!" said Kay. "I wish for music too."
Kay's music came from mermaids and marching soldiers and strange woodland creatures and pipers piping

and fiddlers three,
but Kay's brothers
did not hear it.
"Nobody will listen to me,"
said Kay.
"There must be *somebody*
I can tell about
my magic leaf."

Kay found Granny
sitting shelling peas.
Before Kay could speak,

Granny looked up
and said,
"I see you've caught a magic leaf."

"Oh yes," said Kay.
"It made music and fine clothes
and big bubbles

and a rose with a caterpillar inside
and real sand pies,
but nobody will listen when I tell them.

How did *you* know?"
"Because I caught one once,"
said Granny.
"It did wonderful things,
but everyone was too busy to
listen when I told them."
"Just like me," said Kay.
"Yes dear," said Granny.
"Just like you."